W9-CLU-044

THE MUSIC TEACHER FROM THE BLACK LAGOON

STORY BY
MIKE THALER

PICTURES BY
JARED LEE

Cartwheel BOOKS®

SCHOLASTIC INC.
New York   Toronto   London   Auckland   Sydney
Mexico City   New Delhi   Hong Kong   Buenos Aires

In memory of
Jack Charles Lee
Vietnam 6/11/69
—J.L.

ISBN-13: 978-0-545-07782-8
ISBN-10: 0-545-07782-6

Text copyright © 2000 by Mike Thaler.
Illustrations copyright © 2000 by Jared D. Lee Studio, Inc.

All rights reserved. Published by Scholastic Inc.
SCHOLASTIC, CARTWHEEL BOOKS, and associated logos
are trademarks and/or registered trademarks of Scholastic Inc.

Library of Congress Cataloging-in-Publication Data is available.

10 9 8 7 6 5 4 3 2 1   9 10 11 12 13/0
Printed in the U.S.A. · This edition first printing, April 2009

We have to take a music class this year.
The teacher's name is Miss LaNote.
They say she dresses really weird.

They say Miss LaNote wears armor
and a helmet with horns,
and carries a pitchfork!

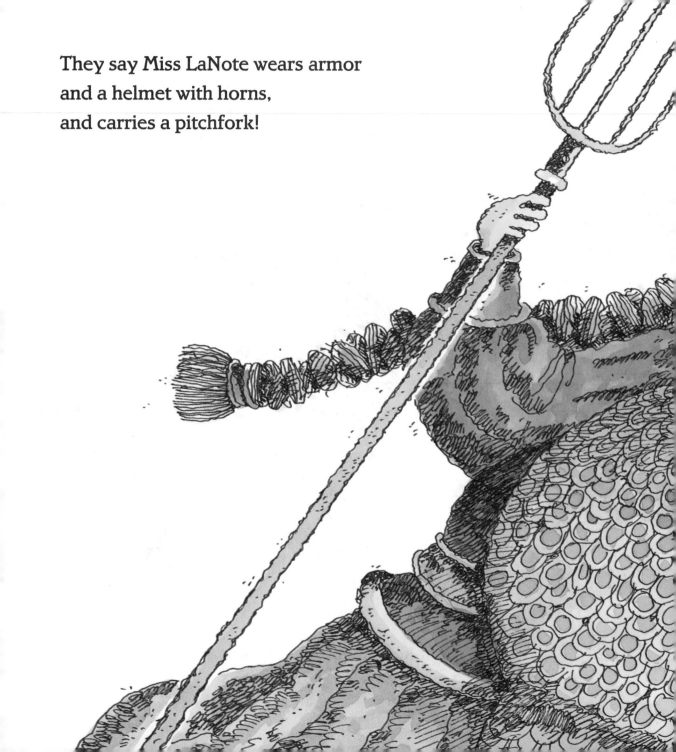

She likes to sing whole operas, really loud, in your ear.
All the kids who wear glasses have to hide them when she hits high C.

Then, they say, Miss LaNote makes *you* sing, too —
in front of the whole class —
in front of the *girls*!

I can sing in the shower, but I can't sing *dry* and *dressed*!

Also, you have to memorize a *million* songs, a *trillion* verses, and a *zillion* notes!

If you sing even *one* wrong,
Miss LaNote zaps you
with her laser baton.

I'm gonna sing solo...SO LOW that no one will hear me.

I heard Miss LaNote uses her *pitchfork*
to keep all the kids on the same key.

They say in her class you don't talk at all.
You have to "sing-sing" everything—
even if you want to go to the bathroom.

Isn't there a prison called *Sing-Sing*?
Music has a lot of *bars*, too.

Then Miss LaNote tells you what kind of voice you have.
There are the *all-toes*, who sing through their toes...

and the *sopran-nose*, who sing through their noses.

I think I'm a *bear-tone* — I sort of growl.

Eric Porter's big brother used to sing with the sopran-nose,
but now he's a bear-tone. They say Miss LaNote stretched
his vocal cords with *tweezers*!

And she forces you to open your mouth as wide as you can. Last year, one kid swallowed his own head!

On top of that, Miss LaNote makes you pick an instrument.

I'm pickin' something small and light 'cause you have to carry your instrument home *every* day.

That's because you have to *practice*.
Instead of playing *baseball*, kids will just be playing *the bass*.
Instead of *hitting* the pitch, they'll be *keeping* the pitch.

They say, if you don't *learn* an instrument, you have to *be* one.
Penny Weber and Doris Foodle were both cymbals,
and Derek Bloom was a drum—ouch!

You also have to learn *the score*.

And it's a lot longer than *Visitors 8 – Home Team 4*.

It looks like a zebra with measles and goes on for pages and pages.

It was all written by dead guys with funny names.

But the worst part is, at the end of the year you have to give a *concert*—in a white shirt—in front of the whole school…your mom…your dad…and all your aunts and uncles!

Well...it's time to face the music. We march in and sit down.

Miss LaNote isn't wearing her helmet today.

She's dressed in musical notes.

She's got musical notes on her shoes, on her dress, and on her ears.

She wants us to sing "Old MacDonald Had a Farm."
I know that song! We get to make all the animal noises!
I'm going to love music, *oink-oink*!